For Tom, David, and Peter M. W.

For Amy and Sandy B. F.

ISBN 0-590-18764-3

Text copyright © 1996 by Martin Waddell.
Illustrations copyright © 1996 by Barbara Firth.
All rights reserved. Published by Scholastic Inc., 555 Broadway, New York,
NY 10012, by arrangement with Candlewick Press.

SCHOLASTIC and associated logos are trademarks and/or registered trademarks
of Scholastic Inc.

12 11 10 9 8 7 6 5   0 1 2/0

Printed in the U.S.A.   09

First Scholastic printing, September 1997

This book was typeset in Columbus MT Semi-bold.
The pictures were done in pencil and watercolor.

YOU AND ME, LITTLE BEAR

Martin Waddell

illustrated by Barbara Firth

Scholastic Inc.

New York   Toronto   London   Auckland   Sydney

Once there were two bears,

Big Bear and Little Bear.

Big Bear is the big bear

and Little Bear is the little bear.

Little Bear wanted to play, but

Big Bear had things to do.

"I want to play!" Little Bear said.

"I have to get wood for the fire," said Big Bear.

"I'll get some, too," Little Bear said.

"You and me, Little Bear," said Big Bear.

"We'll bring the wood in together!"

"What shall we do now?" Little Bear asked.

"I'm going for water," said Big Bear.

"Can I come, too?" Little Bear asked.

"You and me, Little Bear," said Big Bear.

"We'll go for water together."

"Now we can play," Little Bear said.

"I still have to clean up our cave," said Big Bear.

"Well . . . I'll clean up, too!" Little Bear said.

"You and me," said Big Bear. "You clean up your things, Little Bear. I'll take care of the rest."

"I've cleaned up my things, Big Bear!"

Little Bear said.

"That's good, Little Bear," said Big Bear.

"But I'm not finished yet."

"I want you to play!" Little Bear said.

"You'll have to play by yourself,

Little Bear," said Big Bear. "I still

have plenty to do!"

Little Bear went to play by

himself, while Big Bear

continued with the work.

Little Bear played
bear-jump.

Little Bear

played

bear-slide.

Little Bear played

bear-swing.

Little Bear played

bear-tricks with bear-sticks.

Little Bear played bear-stand-on-his-head,

and Big Bear came out to sit on his rock.

Little Bear played bear-run-around-by-himself,

and Big Bear closed his

eyes to think.

Little Bear went to
talk to Big Bear,
but Big Bear was . . .

asleep!

"Wake up, Big Bear!" Little Bear said.

Big Bear opened his eyes.

"I've played all my games

by myself," Little Bear said.

Big Bear thought a minute, then he said,

"Let's play hide-and-seek, Little Bear."

"I'll hide and you seek," Little Bear said,

and he ran off to hide.

"Here I come!" Big Bear called,
and he looked until he
found Little Bear.

Then Big Bear hid, and Little Bear looked.

"I found you, Big Bear!" Little Bear said.

"Now I'll hide again."

They played lots of bear games.

When the sun slipped away through

the trees, they were still playing.

Then Little Bear said, "Let's go

home now, Big Bear."

Big Bear and Little Bear went

home to their cave.

"We've been busy today, Little Bear!"

said Big Bear.

"It was fun, Big Bear," Little Bear

said. "Just you and me playing . . .

ter."